Put Beginning Readers on the Right Track with
ALL ABOARD READING™

The All Aboard Reading series is especially for beginning readers. Written by noted authors and illustrated in full color, these are books that children really and truly *want* to read—books to excite their imagination, tickle their funny bone, expand their interests, and support their feelings. With four different reading levels, All Aboard Reading lets you choose which books are most appropriate for your children and their growing abilities.

Picture Readers—for Ages 3 to 6
Picture Readers have super-simple texts with many nouns appearing as rebus pictures. At the end of each book are 24 flash cards—on one side is the rebus picture; on the other side is the written-out word.

Level 1—for Preschool through First Grade Children
Level 1 books have very few lines per page, very large type, easy words, lots of repetition, and pictures with visual "cues" to help children figure out the words on the page.

Level 2—for First Grade to Third Grade Children
Level 2 books are printed in slightly smaller type than Level 1 books. The stories are more complex, but there is still lots of repetition in the text and many pictures. The sentences are quite simple and are broken up into short lines to make reading easier.

Level 3—for Second Grade through Third Grade Children
Level 3 books have considerably longer texts, use harder words and more complicated sentences.

All Aboard for happy reading!

Special thanks to James F. Romano, Ph.D., Curator,
Department of Egyptian, Classical, and Ancient Middle Eastern Art,
The Brooklyn Museum.
And thanks to Terry Rasberry for photography — S.S.

Photo credits: pp. 29, 35, 48, The Metropolitan Museum of Art; p. 43, UPI/Bettmann.

Library of Congress Cataloging-in-Publication Data

Milton, Joyce.
    Mummies / by Joyce Milton ; illustrated by Susan Swan.
        p.   cm. — (All aboard reading)
    Summary: Explains the Egyptian pharaohs' beliefs about life after death, details the
technique of mummification, and describes pyramids as burial places.
    1. Mummies—Egypt—Juvenile literature. [1. Mummies. 2. Egypt—Antiquities.]
I. Title. II. Series.
DT62.M7M53   1996
932—dc20   96-19295
                                                                                         CIP
                                                                                         AC
ISBN 0-448-41326-4 (GB)   A B C D E F G H I J

ISBN 0-448-41325-6 (pbk)   A B C D E F G H I J

ALL
ABOARD
READING™
Level 2
Grades 1-3

MUMMIES

By Joyce Milton
Illustrated by Susan Swan

Grosset & Dunlap • New York

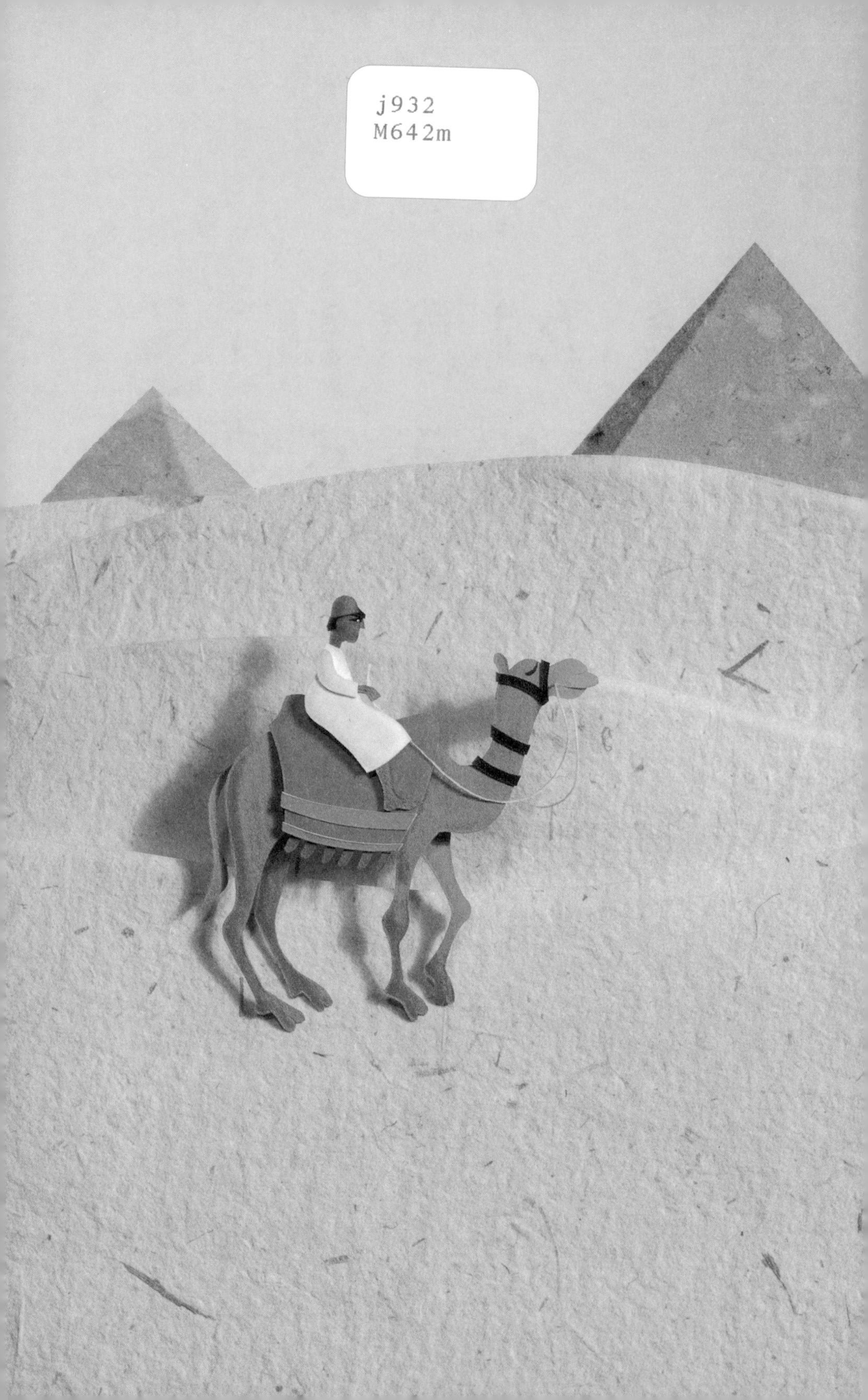

In Egypt giant pyramids
rise above the sand.
Who built them?
And why?

The pyramids were built
thousands of years ago by great kings.
The kings were called pharaohs.
(You say it like this: FA-rows.)
It took 100,000 workers twenty years
to build the biggest pyramid.
But no pharaoh
ever lived in a pyramid.
How could he?
There are no windows
and no doors!
That's because a pyramid
is a tomb.
After a pharaoh died,
his body was put inside it.

Like all Egyptians,

the pharaoh believed in life after death.

His spirit would live on

in the Land of the Dead.

Life there would be just like

life on earth, only better!

In the Land of the Dead,
the pharaoh could do
all the things he loved—
ride, hunt, and fish.
He could even have parties.

But to enjoy
life after death,
the pharaoh still
needed his body.
So his body was made
into a mummy.
A mummy is a body
that has been dried out
like a raisin.
It will not rot away.
King Khufu
(you say it like this: KOO-foo)
was the pharaoh who built
the biggest pyramid of all.

On the day Khufu died,
his family was with him.
So were priests.

Soon after,
a boat took Khufu's body
across the Nile River.

Other priests were waiting

to make the king's body

into a mummy.

It took about seventy days
from beginning to end
to make a mummy.
First, the undertakers
cut open Khufu's body.

14

They left his heart inside.

But they took out his lungs,

liver, stomach, and intestines.

These parts were put into special jars

with lids shaped like animals and gods.

They would be placed in the pyramid

along with the mummy.

Next, the body was packed in natron.

Natron is like salt.

After many weeks in natron,

Khufu's body was all dried out.

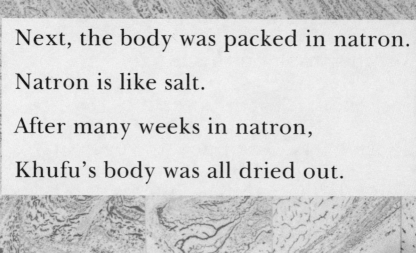

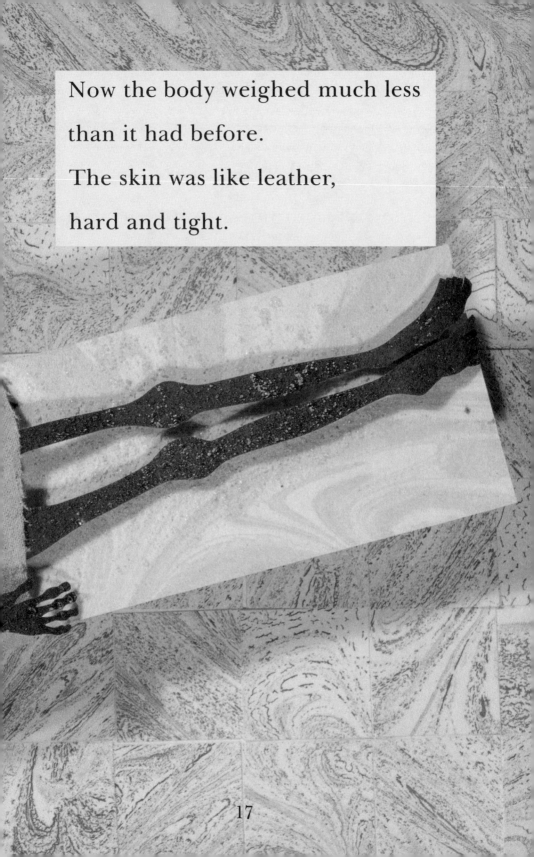

Now the body weighed much less
than it had before.
The skin was like leather,
hard and tight.

The undertakers then
tore fine white cloth into long strips.
They wrapped the strips
around the mummy from head to toe.
Priests in masks watched the work.
They said prayers over the body.
They placed magic charms and jewels
between the strips of cloth.

After the mummy was all wrapped,

the undertakers covered it

with sticky sap from trees.

Once the sap dried,

the mummy was as hard as a statue.

At last, it was time for Khufu's funeral.

His mummy was put in a fancy coffin.

And that coffin was put

in another fancy coffin.

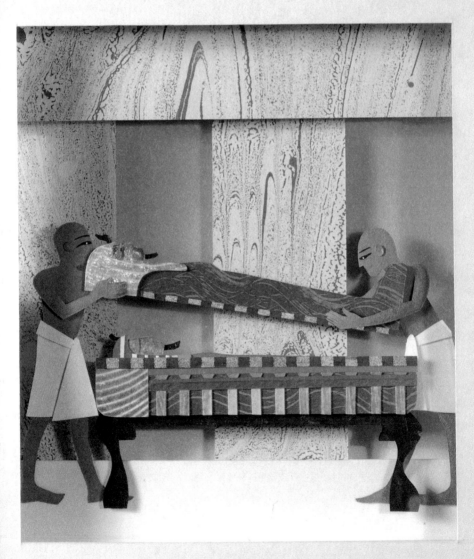

Then Khufu's mummy was placed
on a sled and dragged to his pyramid.
A long parade followed.

Priests said prayers.

Women tore their clothes

and cried out loud.

Deep inside the pyramid,

a hallway led to a small room.

There the priests said

one last prayer for the mummy.

The prayer was called

the "Opening of the Mouth."

Now Khufu would be able

to speak and eat again.

Other rooms in the pyramid
were filled with fancy
furniture and jewels.

The treasures were for Khufu
to enjoy in the afterlife.

When all was in place,

the hallway was plugged

with blocks of stone.

The workers left by a secret passage.

Then the passage was filled

with rocks and walled over.

All this was done

to keep Khufu's mummy

and his treasure safe.

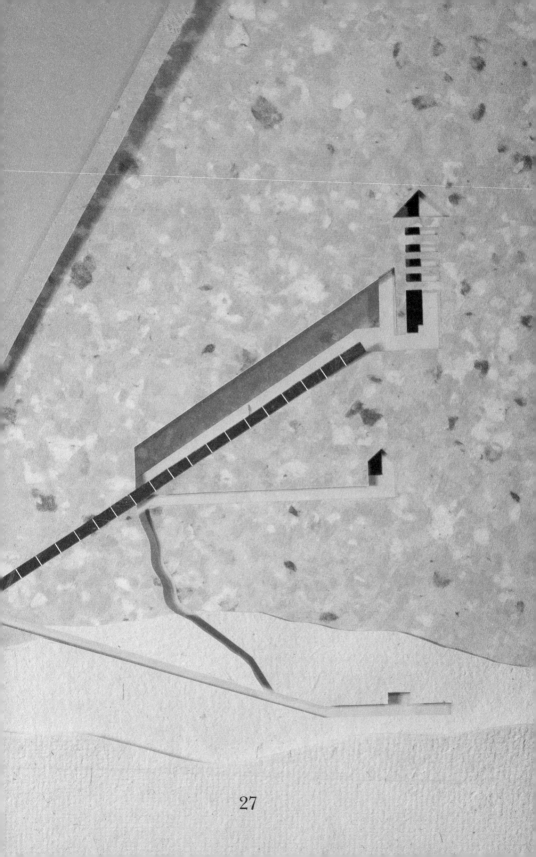

After a while, the pharaohs
stopped building pyramids.
Instead, they built tombs
deep underground.
The mummies in these tombs
looked even more lifelike.
Undertakers put stuffing
under the mummy's skin.
This made its cheeks rounder.
They made fake eyes out of glass
or black-and-white stones.

When the mummy was done,

its face was painted.

Some mummies had fake eyebrows

made of real hair.

This is a fancy mummy wig.

In the beginning,
only kings, queens,
and very important people
were made into mummies.
But as time went on,
more and more people
wanted their bodies
prepared for the next world.
Some people had their pets
made into mummies, too.
One man had two animals
put in his tomb with him—
his dog and his pet baboon.

There were mummies
made of other animals, too,
like bulls and snakes
and even crocodiles.
These were to honor
gods and goddesses
who looked like the animals.

The god Thoth had the head of a bird.

The bird was an ibis.

So ibis mummies were made.

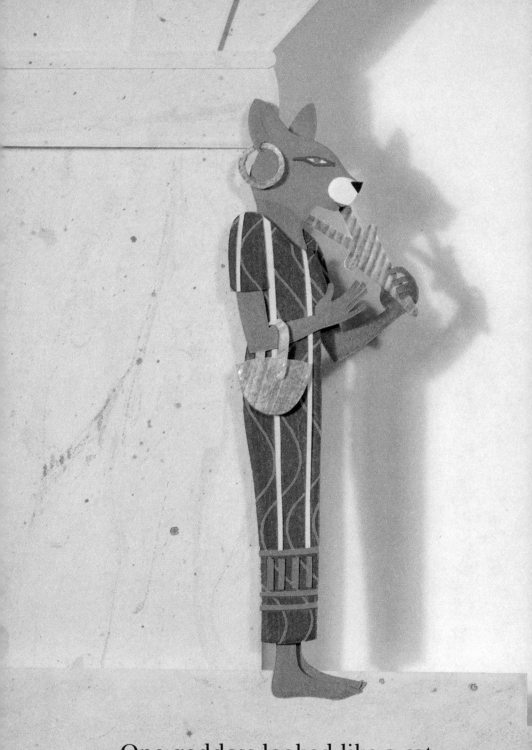

One goddess looked like a cat.

There were temples in her honor
filled with thousands of cat mummies!

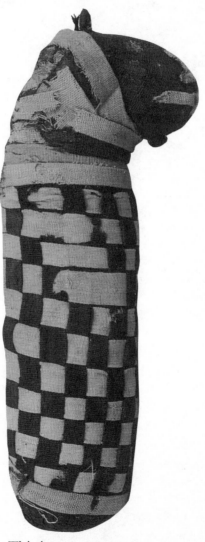

This is one cat mummy.

Once a mummy was buried,

it was supposed to be safe.

But was it?

No!

People robbed the tombs.

They wanted the treasure.

Some robbers even came
to steal the mummies.
Many people
thought mummies
had magic powers.
Travelers came from
far away to find them.

They ground up the mummies
and sold mummy medicine.
They thought eating mummy
powder would make them strong.
Instead, it usually made them sick!

Some travelers brought mummies
home with them.
They unwrapped the mummies
to see what they looked like.
They even sold tickets
to people who wanted to watch.

Today, scientists study mummies.
They want to learn
all they can about them.
This mummy is kept
at a hospital in Boston.
Its name is Padihershef.
But scientists just call him Padi.
Scientists do not even need to
unwrap mummies to study them.
They can use X-rays.
X-rays can show what
diseases people had long ago.

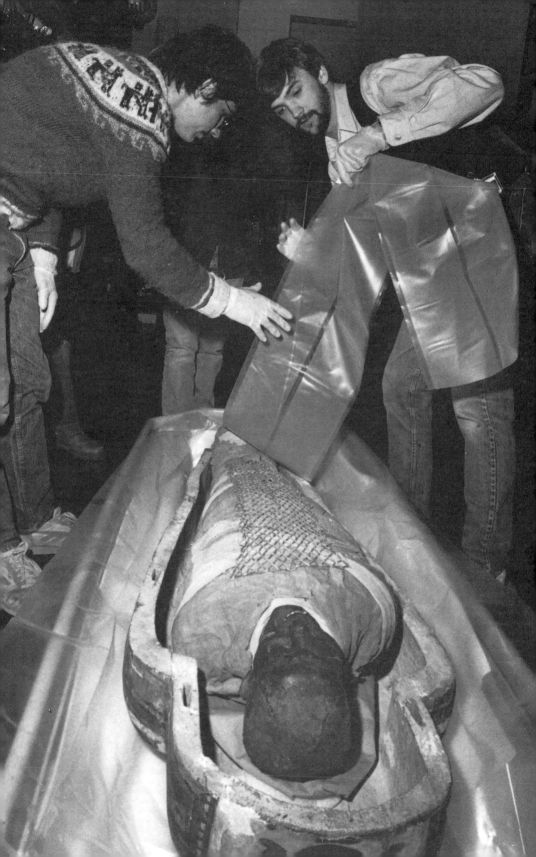

Scientists and explorers

have been searching for mummies

for hundreds of years.

So many have been found.

Can any more be left?

Yes!

Not long ago, scientists found

a huge underground tomb.

It was filled with mummies.

Why was the tomb so big?

It belonged to the children

of a pharaoh.

His name was Ramesses the Great.

(You say it like this: RAM-es-sess.)

Ramesses had more than 100 children!

Who knows?
Under the rocks and sand,
there may be more mummies
waiting to be found!

AUTHOR _Mummies_

TITLE

DATE DUE	BORROWER'S NAME
OCT 28	Alex 101